Book 4

Ick and Crud
The Big Crunch

by Wiley Blevins • illustrated by Jim Paillot

RED CHAIR •PRESS•

Funny Bone Books

and Funny Bone Readers are produced and published by

Red Chair Press LLC   PO Box 333   South Egremont, MA 01258-0333

www.redchairpress.com

About the Author

Wiley Blevins has taught elementary school in both the United States and South America. He has also written over 60 books for children and 15 for teachers, as well as created reading programs for schools in the U.S. and Asia with Scholastic, Macmillan/McGraw-Hill, Houghton-Mifflin Harcourt, and other publishers. Wiley currently lives and writes in New York City.

About the Artist

Jim Paillot is a dad, husband and illustrator. He lives in Arizona with his family and two dogs and any other animal that wants to come in out of the hot sun. When not illustrating, Jim likes to hike, watch cartoons and collect robots.

Publisher's Cataloging-In-Publication Data
(Prepared by The Donohue Group, Inc.)

Names: Blevins, Wiley. | Paillot, Jim, illustrator.
Title: Ick and Crud. Book 4, The big crunch / by Wiley Blevins ; illustrated by Jim Paillot.
Other Titles: Big crunch

Description: South Egremont, MA : Red Chair Press, [2017] | Series: First chapters | Interest age level: 005-007. | Summary: "It's another lazy day in the backyard and Ick isn't too happy to explore the sound in the woods. But Crud has his back - or does he?"--Provided by publisher.

Identifiers: LCCN 2016947354 | ISBN 978-1-63440-206-4 (library hardcover) | ISBN 978-1-63440-207-1 (paperback) | ISBN 978-1-63440-208-8 (ebook)

Subjects: LCSH: Friendship--Juvenile fiction. | Sounds--Juvenile fiction. | Forests and forestry--Juvenile fiction. | Dogs--Juvenile fiction. | CYAC: Friendship--Fiction. | Sound--Fiction. | Forests and forestry--Fiction. | Dogs--Fiction.

Classification: LCC PZ7.B618652 Icb 2017 (print) | LCC PZ7.B618652 (ebook) | DDC [E]--dc23

Printed in the United States of America
0517 1P CGBF17

Table of Contents

1 Follow the Crunch 5

2 Ghost in the Trees 9

3 Busted! 15

4 Wiggle, Squiggle, Stuck . . . 19

5 Waddle Home 23

Meet the Characters

Crud

Ick

Miss Puffy

Bob

Follow the Crunch

"**W**hy are we running?" asked Ick.

"You'll see," said Crud.

They raced through their yard, jumped over the fence, and landed in Mrs. Martin's flower bed, which was still all mud.

"Oh not again," said Crud. "Rats!"

"Rats?" asked Ick. "Where?"

"No, not rats," said Crud, wiping off the mud. "Oh, crud, crud, crud!"

"Why are you yelling your name?" asked Ick. "Did you forget it?" Crud rolled his eyes. "I mean *oh nuts*," he said.

"Now you're making me hungry," said Ick. The two stood up and starting dripping across the yard. Just then a crunching noise drifted in from the woods.

"Did you hear that?" asked Crud.

"Hear what?" asked Ick.

"That crunching sound," said Crud. He pointed to the woods and then took off.

Ick ran double time to keep up with
him. "Why are we running?" asked Ick.

"That crunching sound is our food.
Someone is stealing it."

"Hold the doggie door," said Ick.
He skidded to a stop. "I thought *you*
were eating all our food."

"And why would you think that?" asked
Crud. Ick pointed to Crud's big belly.

"I'm storing up for winter," said Crud.

"But it's only June," said Ick.

He stood on his hind legs and waddled like Crud.

"If you keep walking like that," said Crud, "your legs will freeze that way."

"Nuh-uh," said Ick. Then he dropped down on all four paws. Just in case.

"Let's keep going," said Crud. "And follow that crunch!"

Ghost in the Trees

The two raced to the edge of Mrs. Martin's yard, over another fence, through another yard, around a shed, then down a hill, and across a small garden. But when they got to the edge of the woods, Ick skidded to a stop.

"What's wrong?" asked Crud. "Aren't you coming?"

Ick shook his head. "It's dark in the woods. And there are ghosts."

"Ghosts?" asked Crud. "Ghosts don't live in the woods. They live in basements and attics."

"And old doghouses," said Ick.

"Yes," said Crud. "And old doghouses." Ick gulped.

"Come on," said Crud. "If I see a ghost, I'll grit my teeth and shake my tail and scare it away."

"But ghosts eat little dogs," said Ick.

"You're safe with me," said Crud.

"Are you sure?" asked Ick.

"Have I ever let you down, buddy?" asked Crud. Ick shook his head. Then he put one foot inside the woods. *Hoo... hoo... hoot.*

"What's that?" asked Ick.

"That's just an owl," said Crud.
"Come on you scaredy pup."

"I'm not a scaredy pup," said Ick.
"I'm just… careful." He took two more
steps into the woods. Another *hoot*. Crud's
eyes bugged out. He pointed behind Ick.
And off he ran! Ick followed like a flea
was chewing on his tail.

"Works every time," whispered Crud.
Ick and Crud weaved in and out of the
trees. Tall trees. Skinny trees. Fat trees.
And trees with no leaves. They ran until
they came to a big rock.

Turtle rested in the shade beside it. Ick and Crud knocked on his shell. "Hello, Turtle," said Crud.

"Nice day for a run in the woods," said Ick. Turtle poked his head out and tried to shrug, which is really hard to do in a shell.

"Did you hear a crunch?" asked Crud. Turtle slowly nodded.

"Do you know where it is?" asked Ick. Turtle nodded again, then slid back inside his shell. "What should we do now?" asked Ick.

"I don't know," said Crud.

"Maybe he's calling a friend," said Ick. He leaned in to Turtle's shell.

"Hello?" said Ick.

"That's the wrong end," said Crud.

"Oops," said Ick. He walked to the front of Turtle. "Hello," he yelled again. Ick tapped on Turtle's shell. "Can you tell us where you heard the sound?" Turtle poked out his head. Then he pointed his nose at a large tree. It had a big hole in it.

"A-ha!" said Crud. "Just as I thought. Thanks, Turtle."

Busted!

Crud tiptoed to the tree. Ick tiptoed behind him. Or tried to. *Plop.*

"Get up," whispered Crud.

"It's not easy walking on your toes," moaned Ick. He brushed off the leaves.

"We have to sneak up on that thief," said Crud.

"Thief?" asked Ick.

"Robber. Villain. The Stealer of All That Is Yummy."

"Ahh," said Ick.

"And be quiet," said Crud.

"Got it," yelled Ick.

"*Shhh,*" said Crud.

"*Shhh* to you, too," said Ick.

"Stop it," said Crud.

"Stop what?" asked Ick. Crud put his paw on Ick's nose. He mouthed the words, "Can... you... hear... *that*?"

Ick nodded. The hairs on his tail stood up and curled. Crud leaned next to the hole in the tree and darted his head inside.

A squirrel sat at the bottom stuffing food into his mouth. The squirrel looked up. "Uh-oh," he squeaked.

"Gotcha!" yelled Crud.

"Yeah," yelled Ick. "Busted."

"Where's our food?" asked Crud. The squirrel burped. "Excuse me," he squeaked and covered his mouth. Then he pointed to a small pile.

"That's all that's left?" asked Crud. The squirrel just stared. Then he picked up a nut, threw it at Crud, and dashed out of the tree.

Bonk! Swoooosh! The two watched as
the squirrel raced into the woods, and ran
head-first into another tree. *Splat!*

"Squirrels aren't as smart as they
look," said Ick.

"Not as smart as dogs," said Crud.
"Let's get our food."

Wiggle, Squiggle, Stuck

Crud stuffed his head inside the hole, then he lifted up his body. He wiggled. And squiggled. And turned and churned. But he couldn't squeeze through. So he wiggled back. And squiggled back. And turned and churned back. But he couldn't get out.

"Get me out," yelled Crud.

"What?" asked Ick.

"I'm stuck," said Crud.

"You want a stick?" asked Ick.

"No," yelled Crud. "I'm stuck!"

"Are you stuck?" asked Ick. Crud kicked his legs. "Hey, I think you're stuck, buddy," said Ick. "Let me help you." Ick pulled on Crud's tail.

"Owwwww," yelled Crud.

"That won't work," said Ick. So he pulled on Crud's right leg. Nothing moved. Then he pulled on Crud's left leg. Nothing moved. Finally, he poked Crud's butt. But that was just for fun.

"Owwwww," yelled Crud again.

"Hmmm," said Ick. "What can I do? Maybe..." Ick grabbed both of Crud's legs and he pulled and he grunted and he groaned and he tugged until...

…out popped Crud.

"Thanks," said Crud, landing on top of Ick. "Now go in there and get our food."

"What?" asked Ick.

"Only you can fit," said Crud.

"I'm not going in there," said Ick. "Ghosts live in trees."

"Ghosts?" asked Crud. "Ghosts only live in basements and attics and old doghouses," he said.

"And big trees with holes," said Ick.

"Go!" yelled Crud.

Waddle Home

Crud pushed Ick to the hole in the tree.

Ick tipped his head inside. "It's dark in there," he cried.

"Go!" said Crud

"I think I see a ghost," said Ick.

"Look closer," said Crud. "It's just our pile of food." Ick tipped his head further in the hole. And as he did...

BAM!

Thud! "You okay, buddy?" asked Crud. Ick rolled over and scooted to the corner. He looked around for the glowing eyes of a ghost. But all he spotted was the pile of food.

"Hey Crud," said Ick.

"Yes," said Crud.

"I see our food, but... how will we get it home?"

"Hmmm," said Crud. "Let me think." Crud plopped beside the tree and began thinking. Which is hard to do after a long run in the woods. But a little easier to do when you're sitting. A leaf fell beside him. A bird chirped above him. Two worms crawled over a log. But nothing popped into Crud's head as he slowly dozed off.

Inside, Ick was hard at work doing his own thinking. "I've got it!" he said. "Maybe we should eat all the food here." He popped some food into his mouth because it was such a good idea.

"I hear crunching," said Crud, as he woke up.

"It's *really* yummy," yelled Ick. He kept crunching.

Crud poked his head inside the hole. "Don't eat it all," he said. "Toss some up to me."

"Okay," said Ick. "One for you." Up flew a hunk of food. "And two for me," he whispered.

"One for you," Ick said again. "And three for me," he whispered again.

One… four…

One… five…

One… six…

And so on until all the food was gobbled up.

"We did it!" said Ick. Then he rolled on his back, grabbed his belly, and looked around. The hole in the tree now had nothing in it. *Nada. Zilch.* "It's empty," yelled Ick. *"Empty... Empty..."* bounced off the walls and shot back at him.

"A ghost!" cried Ick. *"GET ME OUT OF HERE!!"*

He lifted his arms and jumped up and down. "Pull, Crud," he yelled. "I'm too young to get eaten by a ghost! I'm too cute to get eaten by a ghost!"

"Hang on, Ick," said Crud. Crud grabbed Ick's arms and he pulled and he tugged and he grunted and he groaned until...

29

...out popped Ick. The two rolled away from the tree and landed beside the knocked-out squirrel. "Oh, no," moaned Ick, as he got up.

"Don't worry about that squirrel," said Crud. "He'll be dreaming about nuts for the rest of the day."

"No," said Ick. "I'm not worried about the squirrel. It's my belly."

"Your belly hurts?" asked Crud.

"*Really* hurts," said Ick.

Crud pointed to Ick's belly. Then Ick stood and waddled.

"Okay," said Ick. "Now it's big. Just like
yours. Are you happy?"

"Let's go home, buddy," said Crud.

"Yes," said Ick. "Let's go home." And
the two waddled through the woods. Tall
trees. Skinny trees. Fat trees. And trees
with no leaves.

Until they came to their doghouses.
New ones. With no ghosts.